Calabash Cat

and his amazing journey

by James Rumford

HOUGHTON MIFFLIN COMPANY   BOSTON 2003

www.houghtonmifflinbooks.com

The text of this book is set in Adobe Caslon.
The illustrations are ink on Bristol board.

The author modeled the Arabic calligraphy in this book after the
handwriting of his Chadian friend Brahim Adoum. Chadian Arabic
is spoken by certain tribes in Chad and, in its simplest form, is used
as a market language in a country where many languages are spoken.
Chadian Arabic is a spoken language and rarely written.

Library of Congress Cataloging-in-Publication Data

Rumford, James, 1948–
Calabash Cat / written and illustrated by James Rumford.
       p. cm.
Summary: A Calabash Cat, living in Africa, sets off to see where
the world ends.
ISBN 0-618-22423-8
[1. Voyages around the world—Fiction. 2. Cats—Fiction.
3. Animals—Fiction. 4. Gourds—Fiction. 5. Africa—Fiction.]
I. Title.
PZ7.R8878 Cal 2003
[E]—dc21
2002151175

Printed in Singapore
TWP 10 9 8 7 6 5 4 3 2 1

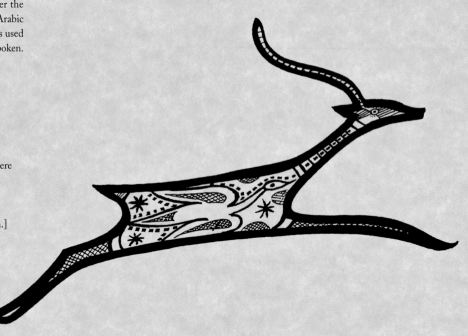

For the Chadian people

IN THE MIDDLE OF AFRICA there lived a calabash cat.

One day, he set off down the road
to see where the world ended.

يوم من الأيام سار وديب يشف مكان
الدنيا كمل ولاكن كان وديب كمل
في كشمر صغيرا ابن بأتو قد وفكر.

When the road stopped
at the edge of the great desert,
Calabash Cat sat down
and thought,
Maybe this
is where
the world
ends.

متھُن دُنیا یکمُل ہنے نُس

شيا كي جمل وصل وقل عجب
كان شيمي كلم لطخ هنا إبن
باتو وقل اركب فوق وانا وصبك
بكان الدنيا يكمّل وهمان ماشربي

Just then a camel came by. He was surprised at how silly Calabash Cat was.

"Climb up on my back, and I will show you where the world ends."

And they walked across the desert.

But when they reached the far side
of the desert where
the grasslands began,
the camel stopped
and said,
"Here, my friend,
is where
the world
ends."

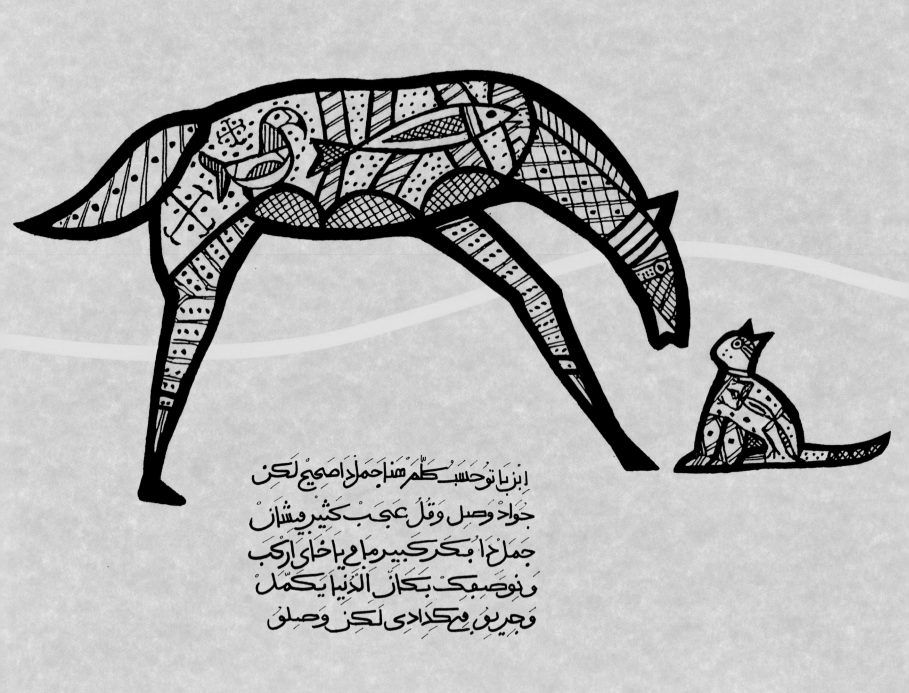

Calabash Cat would have believed the camel had a horse not happened by. The horse was quite surprised at how small-minded the camel had been.

"Climb up on my back, and I will show you where the world ends."

And they galloped across the grasslands.

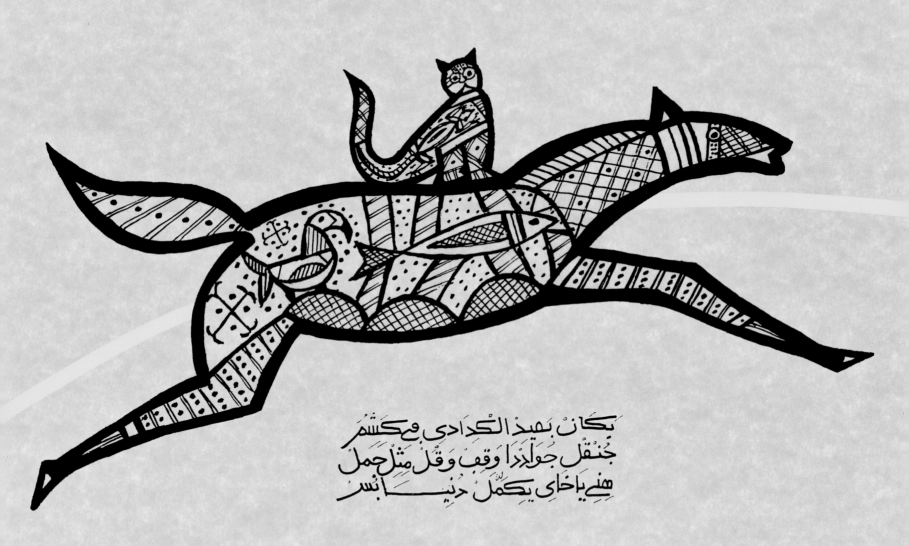

يكان بميذ الكدادى في كشم
جنقل جولمذا وقب وقل مثلاحمل
هنى ياخاى يكمل حنيـا ابسر

But when they reached
the far side of the grasslands
where the jungle began,
the horse stopped
and said proudly,
"Here, my friend,
is where
the world
ends."

إِبْزِيَا تُوحَلَّبِ كَطَمِرُهُنَا جَوَادَ اصِيعُ لَكِنْ

تِيقْرَه وَصِلْ وَقَلْ وَاللّه جَوَادَ امَا

عِنْدَه رَاسِ يَاخَاي ارْكَبْ وَنُوصِبِكَ

بَكَانْ اَلْدِنْيَا يَكَمَّلْ وَجِرُيُومِ حُنْقَلْ

Calabash Cat would have believed the horse had a tiger not shown up. The tiger was quite surprised at how full of nonsense the horse had been.

"Climb up on my back and I will show you where the world ends."

And they bounded through the jungle.

لكن وصلو بعَد الكبير و تيقَنْ
وقِفْ وقَلْ والله يا خاى هذني حَديثاً يكَمَّلْ

But when they reached the ocean,
the tiger stopped and said,
as sure as she could be,
"Here, my friend,
is where
the world
ends."

ابن باتو حلب كلّمر هنا تقره صبيح ولكن
حوت كبير كلّمر له من بعيد وقل يا
خاي كلّمر هنا تقره غلط بسر لازم اركب
في بوق ونوصيفك بكن الدنيا يكمّل
.

Calabash Cat would have believed the tiger had a whale not called from the waves. The whale was quite surprised at how wrong the tiger had been.

"Climb up on my back and I will show you where the world ends."

And they swam across the sea.

وَنَاجِى فِي بَحْرٍ لَكِنْ وَصَلُوا بَكَازٍ بِعِيدْ
البَحْرِ حُوتْ دَا قَلْ دُنْيَا يَكَمَّلْ هِنْ خَلَاصْ

But when they reached the other side
of the ocean,
the whale said,
without hesitating
for one minute,
"Here, my friend,
is where
the world
ends!"

Now when Calabash Cat looked at the miles of land in front of him, he thought how small the whale's world had been, even the tiger's and the horse's and the camel's. He wondered if he would ever see the end of the world.

ووقتِ إبنِ بانو شِبَ كيلومترهِ كثيرْ
في قدامِ وفكرِ دُنيا هنا حوتْ صغيرْ
وسا واسو دُنيا هنا تقرهِ وجوادٌ وجملْ وسِأَلْ
أنا نشبُ يكانْ الدنيا يكملْ ولا .

Just then, an eagle swooped down. The eagle was quite surprised at how foolish everyone had been.

"Climb up on my back and I will show you a world without end."

Up they went—into the great sky.

And Calabash Cat's eyes grew wide with wonder as he flew around the world—over oceans and jungles, grasslands and deserts—back to his home.

شيا كى عقاب طير مى تحت وقل عجب
كل ناس قال ثم عجبي يا خاى اركب فوق
ونوصيك دنيا ال يكمل ما مى وطير و
فوق فى السما الكبير وعيوم هنا ابن
باتو قلاع كبير وقل عجب طير دور دنيا
انثان يقبل بيت هذه خلاص كتبه جمعه الافوز

WHEN I LIVED in the African country of Chad, I bought a beautiful calabash gourd cut in the shape of a cat. The artist who made the cat burned designs into the calabash using a hot iron tool. One day, as I looked at my calabash cat, a story came into my head about a cat who sets off on a journey to find the impossible. I began to imagine the other calabash animals he would meet and started drawing. I also wrote down the story in the Arabic dialect of Chad, because I thought that one day I might want to tell my Chadian friends my calabash story.